GOODBYE

Dee Phillips

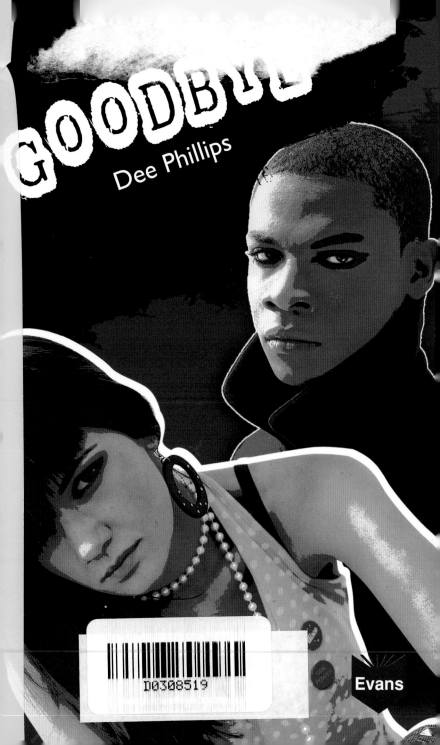

Evans

First published in 2010
by Evans Brothers Limited
2A Portman Mansions
Chiltern Street
London W1U 6NR
UK

Printed in China

British Library Cataloguing in Publication Data
Phillips, Dee, 1967-
> Goodbye. -- (Right now!)
> 1. Couples--Psychology--Fiction. 2. Young adult fiction.
> I. Title II. Series
> 823.9'2-dc22
> ISBN-13: 9780237541941

Developed & Created by Ruby Tuesday Books Ltd

Project Director – Ruth Owen
Head of Design – Emma Randall
Designer – Trudi Webb
Editor – Frances Ridley
Consultant – Lorraine Petersen, Chief Executive of NASEN
© Ruby Tuesday Books Limited 2010

ACKNOWLEDGEMENTS

With thanks to Lorraine Petersen, Chief Executive of NASEN for her help in the development and creation of these books.

Images courtesy of Shutterstock

While every effort has been made to secure permission to use copyright material, the publishers apologise for any errors or omissions in the above list and would be grateful for notification of any corrections to be included in subsequent editions.

I was with Lloyd for three years.
I wanted to be with Lloyd forever.
But it all went wrong.

GOODBYE

It's Thursday night.
I'm at the cinema with Joe.
He's buying the popcorn.
I'm buying the tickets.

I pay for the tickets.
Then I wait for Joe.
Suddenly, I feel something.

I feel someone watching me.

5

I turn around.
My heart starts to thump.

It's
LLOYD

Lloyd is watching me.

I turn away.
I feel like I'm going to cry.
I look back, but Lloyd has gone.

Please stop, Lloyd.
I'm with Joe now.

Joe walks up to me.
He looks worried.
Joe says, "What's up, Lucy?"
I try to smile.

I was with Lloyd for three years.
But it all went wrong.
Now I'm with Joe.
But Lloyd is always watching me.

Joe walks me home.
He takes my hand.
He says, "I really care about you, Lucy."
He wants me to say something nice.
I say, "Bye Joe. Thanks for the popcorn."

It's Friday night.
We're at a party.
I'm dancing with Joe.
Joe goes to kiss me.

Suddenly I see Lloyd in the doorway.
He's watching me.

My heart starts to thump.
I turn my head away.
Joe says, "What's up, Lucy?"

I look back at
the doorway but
Lloyd has gone.

Please stop, Lloyd.
I'm with Joe now.

It's Sunday morning.
I meet Joe in town.
We go for a coffee.

I'm having a good time.
Joe makes me laugh again and again.

Suddenly, I feel something.

I feel someone watching me.

19

I look out of the window.
Lloyd is standing in the street.
He is watching us.
I look away.

Joe says,
"Shall we go to the park?"
I feel like I am going to cry.
I say, "I want to go home."
Joe looks so sad.

Joe walks me home.
He takes my hand.
He says, "I really care
about you, Lucy."

I want to say something nice but I feel sure Lloyd is watching us. Somewhere.

So I say, "See you soon, Joe."

I lie on my bed.
Why did it all have to go wrong?

Mum knocks on the door.
She says, "What's up, Lucy?"

I know I have to tell her.

I say, "Everywhere I go, Lloyd is there."

Mum says, "I know Lucy. But you have
to move on."

I start to cry.

I say, "Lloyd won't let me go, Mum."

Mum gives a sad little smile.

She says, "You must let Lloyd go, too, Lucy."

I was with Lloyd for three years.
I wanted to be with Lloyd forever.

But it all went wrong.

I'm with Joe now.
I like Joe a lot.
I know Mum is right.
I have to move on.
I have to tell Lloyd.

I'm sorry Lloyd but I'm with Joe now.

I know where to
find Lloyd.
I know where to go.
I've not been to this
place before.
I didn't want to
see Lloyd again.

I wanted to be with Lloyd forever.
But it all went wrong.
Lloyd got ill.

It happened so fast.

Lloyd said, "I'll always be there for you, Lucy."

I find the place.
I say, "Hi there. I'm sorry
it's been so long."

"I have something for you."

I sit with Lloyd.

But I can't say the words.

So I write them down.

I will always love you Lloyd.

But I have to let you go.

And you have to let me go.

It was the best.

Goodbye.

Lx

GHOST WRITER
ON YOUR OWN

Imagine you are Lloyd. Write a letter or a poem to Lucy.
Think about:

- How Lloyd might be feeling –
  sad, jealous, angry,
  protective….
- What he wants Lucy to do –
  forget about him, remember
  him, split up with Joe…
- How he wants Lucy to feel –
  comforted, guilty, tormented,
  angry…

BOOK TALK
WITH A PARTNER

Discuss the book with your partner.

- Did you guess that Lloyd was dead?
- Did you think that Lloyd was stalking Lucy?
- What clues are there in the book
  about what had happened?
- How do the pictures help to tell
  the story?
- How did the ending make you feel?

WHAT DID LUCY SEE?
IN A GROUP

What is it that Lucy sees?
Is it really Lloyd's ghost?
Or does she see Lloyd
because she feels guilty?
Or is it something else
altogether?

Choose someone in your group to be Lucy and put her in the
hot seat! Ask her questions to find out what she thinks was
going on.

A VISITOR FROM THE DEAD
ON YOUR OWN / WITH A PARTNER / IN A GROUP

Find out about other
ghostly visitors in books
and movies.
For example:

Marley's ghost in
A Christmas Carol.
Sam's ghost in the
movie *Ghost.*

- Who did the ghost visit? Why?
- What did the person do after he or she had
  seen the ghost?

Create a scene about a ghost visiting a person.
You could write it, draw it, or act it out.

IF YOU ENJOYED THIS BOOK, TRY THESE OTHER **RiGHT NOW!** BOOKS.

Steve hates what he sees in the mirror. Lizzie does, too. Their lives would be so much better if they looked different.

Mark's fighter jet is under attack. There's only one way to escape...

Alisha's online messages to new girl Sam get nastier and nastier. Will anyone help Sam?

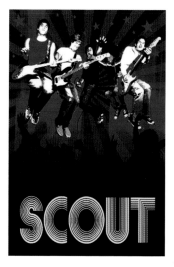

It's Saturday night.
Two angry guys. Two knives.
There's going to be a fight.

Tonight is the band's big
chance. Tonight, a record
company scout is at their gig!

Ed's platoon is under attack.
Another soldier is in danger.
Ed must risk his own life to
save him.

It's just an old, empty house.
Lauren must spend the night
inside. Just Lauren and the
ghost...

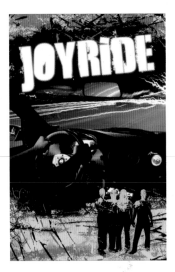

Dan sees the red car.
The keys are inside. Dan says
to Andy, Sam and Jess,
"Want to go for a drive?"

Today is Carl's trial with
City. There's just one place
up for grabs. But today,
everything is going wrong!

Sophie hates this new town.
She misses her friends.
There's nowhere to skate!

Tonight, Vicky must make a
choice. Stay in London with
her boyfriend Chris. Or start
a new life in Australia.